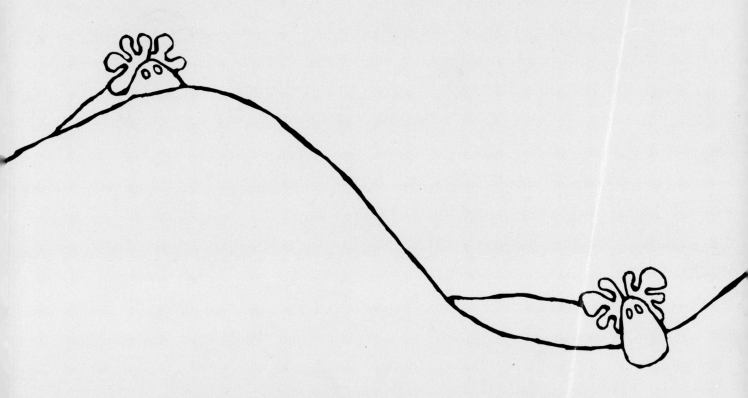

THiS BOOK iS DEDiCATED TO MY gRANDCHiLDREN
AND TO LiTTLE KiDS EVErYWHERE WHO UNDErSTAND CLEARLY
THAT MOOSE ARE PEOPLE TOO.

I was sitting in an airplane staring out at the clouds when
"Mooses Come Walking" came to me. I had never thought or wrote about
moose before. When I began reciting "Mooses" in concert, it seemed to me
that the poem would be wonderful for children. People would approach me
after the shows and want to know where they could get a copy of it for their
kids. I finally agreed to let "Mooses" become a book, and there was no one I
knew who could provide the illustrations more wonderfully than Alice Brock.
I've been a record, a movie, a performer, and part of a TV show, but I have
never been a book about moose. . . . I'm thrilled.

Arlo Guthrie, 1995

Printed in Hong Kong.

Library of Congress Cataloging-in-Publication Data
Guthrie, Arlo.
Mooses come walking/poem by Arlo Guthrie; illustrated by Alice Brock.
32p.   20.3 x 20.3cm.
Summary: Describes the activities of moose as they walk and wander,
even looking in the window at you lying in bed.

ISBN 0-8118-1051-8

[1. Moose – Fiction. 2. Stories in rhyme.] I. Brock, Alice May, 1941-   ill. II. Title.
PZ8.3.G963Mo 1995
[Fic] – dc20   95-15441   CIP AC

Distributed in Canada by Raincoast Books
8680 Cambie Street, Vancouver, B.C. V6P 6M9

10 9 8 7 6 5 4 3 2

Chronicle Books
275 Fifth Sreet San Francisco, CA 94103

MOOSES
COME WALKING

BY ARLO GUTHRIE

ILLUSTRATED BY ALICE M. BROCK

CHRONICLE BOOKS

SAN FRANCISCO

MOOSES COME WALKING

UP OVER THE HiLL

MOOSES COME WALKING

THEY RARELY STAND STILL.

WHEN MOOSES COME WALKING

THEY WALK WHERE THEY WILL

AND MOOSES COME WALKING

UP OVER THE HILL.

MOOSES LOOK INTO

YOUR WiNDOW AT NiGHT,

THEY LOOK TO THE LEFT

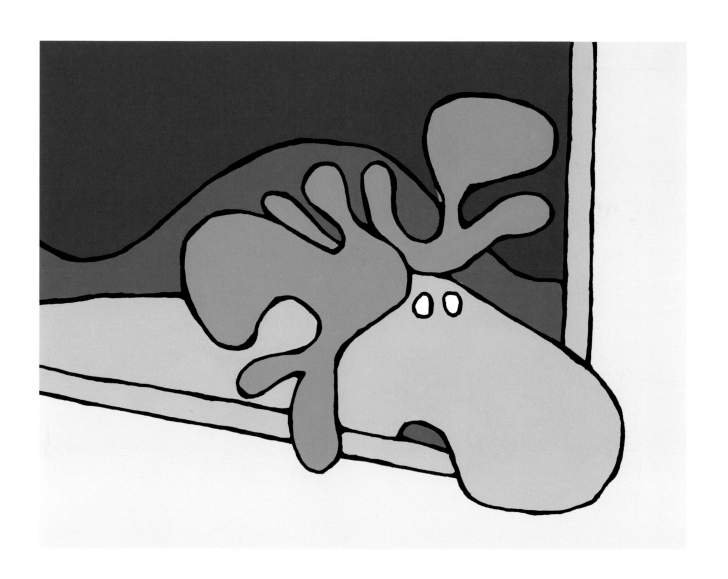

AND THEY LOOK TO THE RiGHT.

THE MOOSES ARE SMILING

THEY THINK IT'S A ZOO

AND THAT'S WHY THE MOOSES

LIKE LOOKING AT YOU.

SO, iF YOU SEE MOOSES

WHILE LYING IN BED

IT'S BEST JUST TO LAY THERE

PRETENDING YOU'RE DEAD.

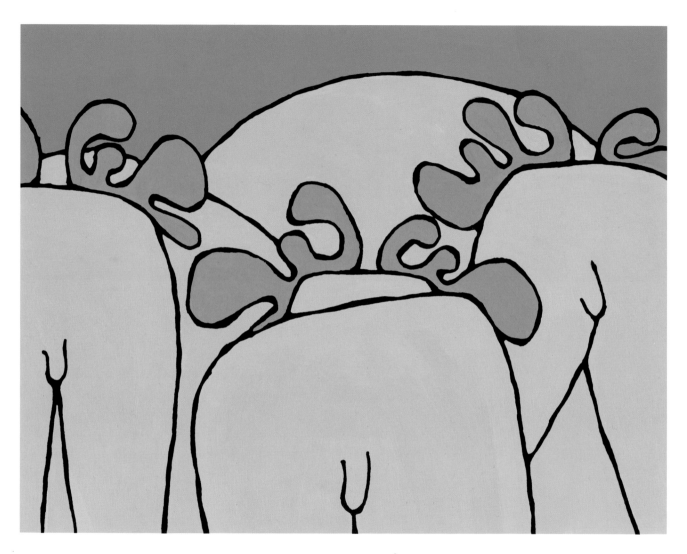

THE MOOSES WILL LEAVE

AND YOU'LL GET THE THRILL

OF SEEING THE MOOSES

go over the HiLL.

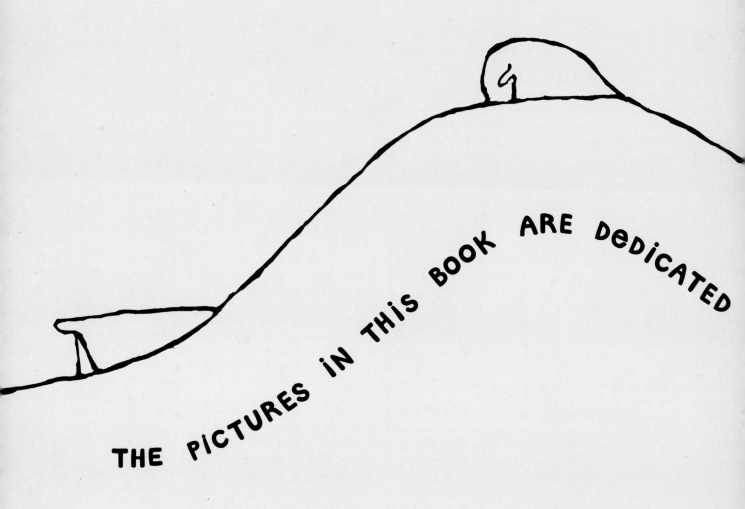

THE PICTURES IN THIS BOOK ARE DEDICATED